READING CORNER
PHONICS

D0347489

Frog and the Bath

FOR SALE
WITHDRAWN
FROM STOCK

Practising CVCC and
CCVC plus polysyllabic words

BOROUGH OF POOLE

550504014 0

First published in 2007 by
Franklin Watts
338 Euston Road
London
NW1 3BH

Franklin Watts Australia
Level 17/207 Kent Street
Sydney
NSW 2000

Text © Sue Graves 2007
Illustration © Daniel Howarth 2007

The rights of Sue Graves to be identified as the author
and Daniel Howarth as the illustrator of this Work have
been asserted in accordance with the Copyright, Designs
and Patents Act, 1988.

All rights reserved. No part of this publication may be
reproduced, stored in a retrieval system, or transmitted
in any form or by any means, electronic, mechanical,
photocopy, recording or otherwise, without the prior
written permission of the copyright owner.

A CIP catalogue record for this book is available
from the British Library.

ISBN: 978 0 7496 7129 7 (hbk)
ISBN: 978 0 7496 7316 1 (pbk)

Series Editor: Jackie Hamley
Series Advisors: Dr Barrie Wade, Dr Hilary Minns
Series Designer: Peter Scoulding

Printed in China

Franklin Watts is a division of
Hachette Children's Books.

BOROUGH OF POOLE	
550504014 O	
JF	£3.99
2008	PETERS

PHONICS

Frog and the Bath

by
Sue Graves

Illustrated by
Daniel Howarth

W
FRANKLIN WATTS
LONDON•SYDNEY

Sue Graves
"My son loved putting on a snorkel and mask to have a bath. It was the only way we could get him to wash!"

Daniel Howarth
"Have you ever tried drawing a frog? They just won't sit still ... and they smell! The ducks were much better behaved."

Frog was at the pond.

The pond had a lot of mud in it.

"I like mud!" said Frog.

Splash!

Frog went in the pond.

"I like to hop in
mud!" said Frog.

11

"And I like to jump
in mud!" said Frog.

13

"You smell!" said Duck.

14

"No," said Frog.

"I *stink!*"

"Come in, Frog!" said Mum.

Frog went in.

"You smell!" said Mum.

18

"No," said Frog. "I *stink*!"

Mum got the bath plug.

"Get in the bath!" she said.

"No!" said Frog.

21

"Yes!" said Mum.

"No!" said Frog. "I like mud on me. It is fun to stink!"

Mum had a think.

She got the junk box.

25

"This is for you," she said.

"Yes!" said Frog.

Splash! Frog got in the bath.

"This is fun!" said Frog.

"Yes," said Mum with a grin.

Notes for parents and teachers

READING CORNER PHONICS has been structured to provide maximum support for children learning to read through synthetic phonics. The stories are designed for independent reading but may also be used by adults for sharing with young children.

The teaching of early reading through synthetic phonics focuses on the 44 sounds in the English language, and how these sounds correspond to their written form in the 26 letters of the alphabet. Carefully controlled vocabulary makes these books accessible for children at different stages of phonics teaching, progressing from simple CVC (consonant-vowel-consonant) words such as "top" (t-o-p) to trisyllabic words such as "messenger" (mess-en-ger). READING CORNER PHONICS allows children to read words in context, and also provides visual clues and repetition to further support their reading. These books will help develop the all important confidence in the new reader, and encourage a love of reading that will last a lifetime!

If you are reading this book with a child, here are a few tips:

1. Talk about the story before you start reading. Look at the cover and the title. What might the story be about? Why might the child like it?

2. Encourage the child to reread the story, and to retell the story in their own words, using the illustrations to remind them what has happened.

3. Discuss the story and see if the child can relate it to their own experience, or perhaps compare it to another story they know.

4. Give praise! Small mistakes need not always be corrected. If a child is stuck on a word, ask them to try and sound it out and then blend it together again, or model this yourself. For example "wish" w-i-sh "wish".

READING CORNER PHONICS covers two grades of synthetic phonics teaching, with three levels at each grade. Each level has a certain number of words per story, indicated by the number of bars on the spine of the book:

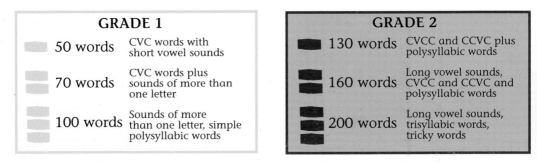

GRADE 1		GRADE 2	
50 words	CVC words with short vowel sounds	130 words	CVCC and CCVC plus polysyllabic words
70 words	CVC words plus sounds of more than one letter	160 words	Long vowel sounds, CVCC and CCVC and polysyllabic words
100 words	Sounds of more than one letter, simple polysyllabic words	200 words	Long vowel sounds, trisyllabic words, tricky words